Dear Caitlin, Caeden & Dacy

Thank you for your support,

Love always,

Janice

Published by Janice Elizabeth Berte

ISBN 978-0692276068

DEDICATION

My sincere dedication goes to my husband Peter for being my best friend in this long awaited endeavor. Also, to Dr. Harter and Dr. Beilin at Framingham State University who inspired me with their incredible knowledge and talent in teaching English Literature. And to all of the children in the world who have suffered separation from their friends at school and simply needed acceptance, love and guidance in becoming happy and healthy children.

MY SINCERE APPRECIATION GOES TO THE FOLLOWING:

Brian Antifonario, my Illustrator and friend. What an interesting ride this has been in completing this book.

Joe Walker, my tech expert who helped me through this long process, and is an asset to this book project.

Thank you so much,

Janice

Once upon a time there was a little boy named Michael. Michael was a beautiful boy who just wanted to fit in with the other kids at school.

One day when Michael wanted to play soccer at recess, he was picked last by the soccer captain, Kevin.

Kevin was the athletic team captain who was also a bully. As the two teams played soccer, Kevin would say mean things to Michael. He would sometimes yell "Hurry up fatso!"

Kevin's name calling hurt Michael so bad that after a couple of games, Michael ran away crying from the soccer field.

Michael ran into the school and one of his teachers, Mrs. Clark saw Michael crying. She came in and sat next to him, and asked him "what is wrong, Michael?"

At first, Michael would say nothing since he didn't want to get Kevin into trouble. Michael also felt embarrassed that he was chubby. Mrs. Clark tried many times in asking Michael what was wrong but Michael never told her.

After meeting Mrs. Clark, Michael went into the cafeteria to have lunch where he would sit by himself and all the other kids would sit with Kevin. Sometimes, Michael would cry at the lunch table.

One day when it was raining out, all the kids had to stay inside and climb a rope in gym class. This made Michael feel bad since he knew he couldn't climb the rope. When Mr. Arnold, the gym teacher asked Michael to start climbing, he fell off quickly. Once again Kevin would yell hurtful comments to Michael saying, "Michael can't climb anything." Mr. Arnold told Kevin to stop the name calling immediately.

Finally, after gym class, Mrs. Clark walked by and saw Michael sitting alone at the back steps of the school sobbing. Mrs. Clark came over to Michael and again asked Michael "what is wrong" and she insisted that he tell her. "It is the only way I can help you get better," said Mrs. Clark.

Michael finally told Mrs. Clark that Kevin called him mean names all the time. "It really hurts my feelings Mrs. Clark," said Michael. "Kevin calls me fatso and other mean names and I can't take it anymore. I just want to fit in and be liked." Mrs. Clark told Michael that she would fix everything and things will get better soon.

So, Mrs. Clark called Michael's parents to have them come to the school. They all sat down in her office and discussed what was happening to Michael and why he never went out to recess. Michael turned to his Mother and said, "Why am I so fat, Mommy?" Michael's Mother said to him, "you are not fat, Michael."

The teacher asked Michael to tell his parents who called him those names, and Michael had to finally confess as to who it was. It was so hard for Michael to share this information, but he knew that he had a lot of support and felt relieved that it was out in the open.

While Mrs. Clark and Michael's parents discussed Michael's bullying, they also discussed some ways for Michael to get healthier. Mrs. Clark asked the Gym Teacher to join them in the meeting.

After meeting with Michael's parents, Mr. Arnold, the Gym Teacher said he could meet with Michael a couple times per week after school to walk and run around the school track.

Mr. Arnold said he would go over the proper meal plan with Michael so he knew the good food from the bad food. They filled out a personalized meal plan to help him remember what to eat.

When they were finished, Mr. Arnold said, "Here is your daily menu plan that will work for you in order for you to lose some weight."

MY HEALTHY DAILY MENU

BREAKFAST
Oat meal with fruit

Juice

Whole Wheat Bagel

LUNCH
Chicken Sandwich with tomato, lettuce, low fat cheese, skim milk and an apple

DINNER
Turkey Meatloaf

Broccoli and mashed potatoes

Skim milk

AM SNACK
celery sticks with orange

PM SNACK
popcorn

When Michael got home from school, his parents had a delicious snack plate of celery sticks and cut up apples.

The next day in the Principal's office, Kevin had to apologize to Michael for calling him names and was told by the Principal that he would be suspended from school if it happened again.

Kevin also had to write a letter to Michael and his parents apologizing to them. The letter promised he would not call Michael mean names any more.

Mr. Arnold decided to have a special health day at school which displayed all the good foods in the gymnasium. There were tables of nutritional items like apples, oranges, bananas, broccoli, potatoes, carrots, eggs, turkey, hummus, berries, yogurt and whole grains.

All the kids gathered around the tables to see how they can make better choices between the good foods and bad foods.

They didn't want to eat any of the unhealthy cotton candy, greasy pizza and hamburgers, french fries and candy bars any more.

The kids in the school loved the health day and they all got to sample various good foods. Mr. Arnold showed them that they will have more energy, live longer and do much better in school by eating right and exercising.

The cafeteria staff started making healthy meals and the children at the school started winning at sports and getting better grades, but more importantly the children became very healthy.

Michael was so excited about eating good foods that his parents changed their own eating habits and they all decided to start an exercise routine. They thought an after dinner bike ride would be good for all of them to enjoy.

After a short time, Michael lost his weight and started sitting with the other kids in the cafeteria. Every day he brought fruits, salads and home-made nutritious sandwiches to school which gave him more energy.

One day, Kevin nervously walked over to Michael at recess and asked him, "Michael, would you like to be on my team?" Michael said "yes, but you will have to ask the other chubby kids to be on our team. I want you to be fair to all of us." Kevin thought about that and said, "You are right and I will be fair to everyone."

That day a lesson was learned by all that everyone needs to accept everyone's differences. The soccer game they played was the most fun they had in a long time and everyone made new friends.

Janice Elizabeth Berte is a Writer. She loves to travel and lives in Massachusetts with her husband, Peter. Jan's writing has been in *Real Simple* magazine, *Betterafter50.com*, *Framingham Life* magazine, and many other publications. Her interviews include Celebrity Chef Jacques Pepin, Chief "Silent Drum" Lopez of the Wampanoag Tribe, and Bob Palmer, President of Digital Equipment Corporation. She is a recipient of the Historical Award from Framingham State University. To reach Janice, email her at: jberte@verizon.net

Born 1962 in Lowell, Massachusetts, Brian is an award winning fine art painter, has been doing art ever since he could hold an oversized Crayon, and teaches painting socially and privately in Massachusetts.

Brian's fine art paintings, and digital graphics can be seen at www.Etsy.com/shop/AntifonarioGallery.

34730062R10017

Made in the USA
Charleston, SC
15 October 2014